Frederick Douglass

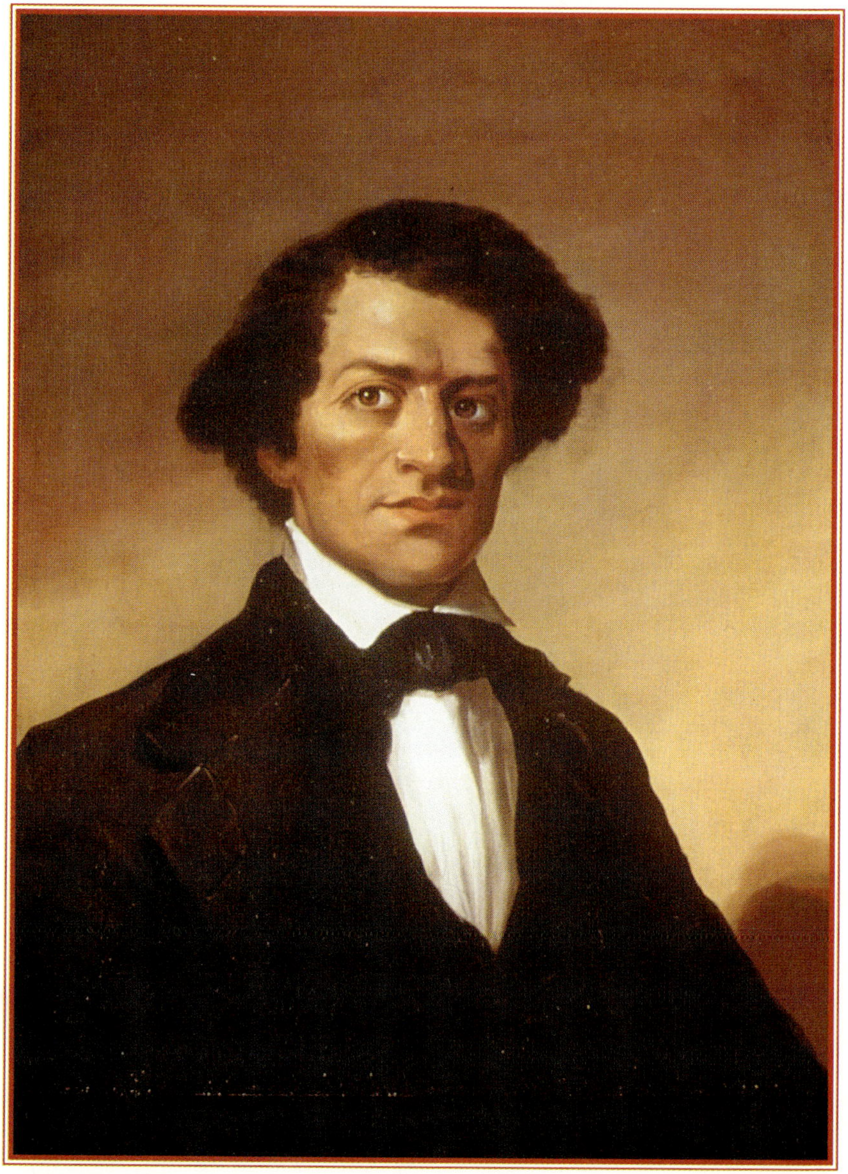

FREDERICK DOUGLASS

By Mona Kerby

A FIRST BOOK
FRANKLIN WATTS
New York / Chicago / London / Toronto / Sydney

To my new friends at Western Maryland College in Westminster, Maryland, and to my old friends at J. B. Little Elementary School in Arlington, Texas.

Cover illustration by Gil Ashby
Photographs copyright ©: The Bettmann Archive: pp. 2, 15, 18, 21, 32, 43, 45, 47, 57; The Metropolitan Museum of Art: p. 8 (Gift of Edgar William and Bernice Chrysler Garbisch, 1963, #63.201.3), 48 (Gift of Mr. and Mrs. Carl Stoeckel, 1897, #97.5); North Wind Picture Archives, Alfred, Me.: pp. 10, 25, 40; New York Public Library, Picture Collection: pp. 13, 27, 30, 34, 50; Moorland-Spingarn Center, Howard University: p. 37 (#2256); New York Public Library, Schomburg Center: p. 39; American Antiquarian Society: p. 42; National Park Service, Frederick Douglass National Historical Site: pp. 53, 56; Historical Society of Washington, D.C., CHS Collection: p. 54.

Library of Congress Cataloging-in-Publication Data

Kerby, Mona
    Frederick Douglass / Mona Kerby
    p. cm.—(First books)
    Includes bibliographical references and index.
    ISBN 0-531-20173-2
    1. Douglass, Frederick, 1817?–1895—Juvenile literature. 2. Abolitionists—United States—Biography—Juvenile literature. 3. Afro-Americans—Biography—Juvenile literature. 4. Slaves—United States—Biography—Juvenile literature. [1. Douglass, Frederick, 1817?–1895. 2. Abolitionists. 3. Afro-Americans—Biography.] I. Title. II. Series.
E449. D75K47   1994
973.8' 092—dc20
[B]   94-15 CIP AC

Copyright © 1994 by Mona Kerby
All rights reserved
Printed in the United States of America
6 5 4 3 2 1

CONTENTS

INTRODUCTION   7

1   EARLY YEARS   11

2   BALTIMORE SLAVE   17

3   FIELD SLAVE   23

4   ESCAPE   29

5   ABOLITIONIST   36

| **6** | CIVIL WAR | 44 |
| **7** | FINAL YEARS | 52 |

FOR FURTHER READING 59

INDEX 61

INTRODUCTION

In the heat of the afternoon, a six-year-old boy and his grandmother reached the end of their 12-mile (19-km) walk. At a big house, the woman turned off the road and headed toward some cabins. Children of all colors ran out to them—"black, brown, copper-colored, and nearly white."

She pointed to the boy's brother and his two sisters. He had never met them before. "Go play," she said softly.

Instead, the little boy stood alone and watched. Later, one of the children called out, "Fed, Fed, grandmamma gone!"

Painted by an unknown artist sometime around 1825, *The Plantation* shows plantation life without any of the cruelties.

He ran to the kitchen. She wasn't there. He ran to the end of the path. She was gone. Years later, he wrote, "I fell upon the ground and wept a boy's bitter tears."

On that August night in 1824, the little boy curled up in a small kitchen closet and cried himself to sleep. It was the first time he knew that he was a slave.

* * *

Slavery, the act of owning people and forcing them to work, has been practiced since prehistoric times. From 1500 to 1800, ten million black Africans were shipped as slaves to North and South America. In the United States, most of these slaves worked on plantations in the South.

While three out of four southern families never owned any slaves, this was not true for wealthy landowners. They bought hundreds of slaves to work on plantations, raising crops such as sugar, cotton, wheat, tobacco, and rice.

Some people said slavery was wrong. Some said it wasn't. Some people didn't care one way or the other.

One thing was for certain. On that summer evening long ago, the young boy's cries went unanswered. But he didn't forget. He knew slavery was wrong.

When he grew up—tall and handsome, with a powerful voice and powerful words—he spoke out. This time, people listened. By telling *his* story, Frederick Augustus Bailey Douglass helped to change the *history* of the world.

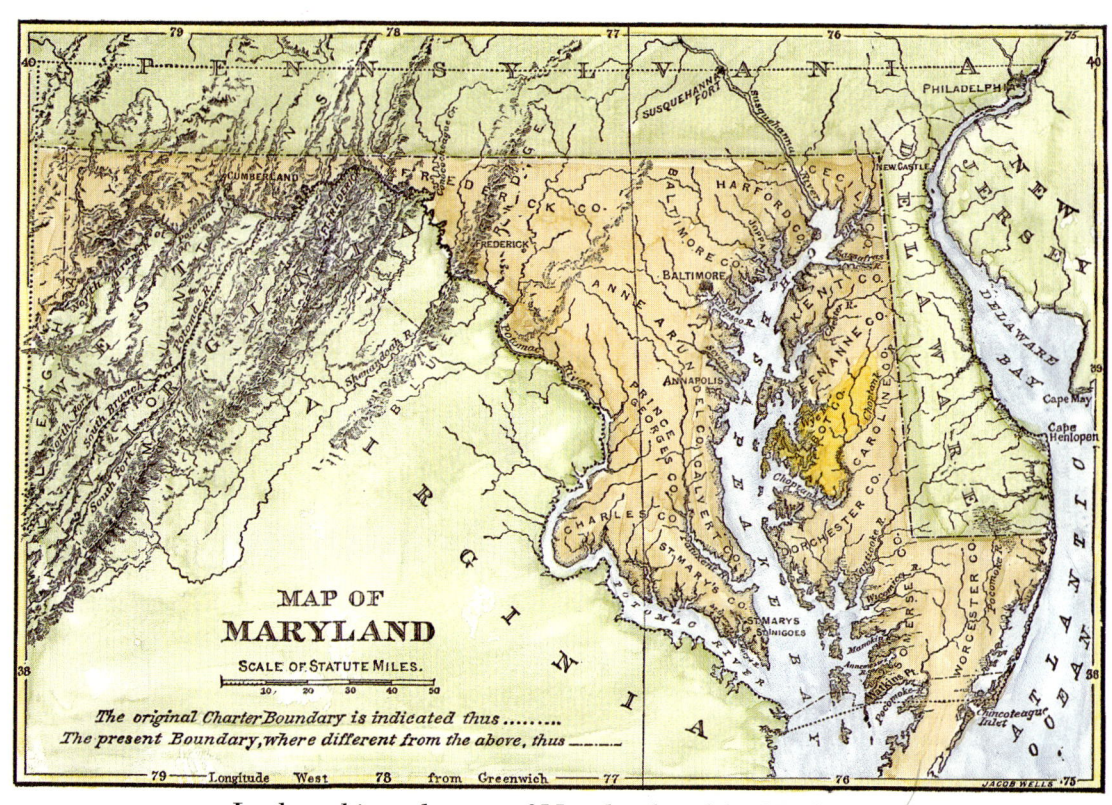

Look at this early map of Maryland and find Talbot County, the birthplace of Frederick Douglass.

EARLY YEARS

Frederick Augustus Bailey was born on the banks of Tuckahoe Creek in Talbot County, Maryland. He never knew his birthday. When Frederick grew up, he celebrated on Valentine's Day, because as near as he could figure out, he was born sometime in February 1817. Actually, he was born in 1818, but this was a fact he never discovered.

His mother, Harriet Bailey, was a slave who worked on another farm. She died when he was seven. Frederick had seen her only a few times in his life.

His father was a white man. That much was admitted;

Frederick's skin was light in color. Some whispered that his father was the man who owned him, Aaron Anthony. Others thought Frederick's father might be Anthony's boss, the owner of the plantation, Colonel Edward Lloyd. Frederick never knew. No one claimed him for a son.

As a young child, Frederick lived deep in the woods with his grandparents, several young cousins, and an uncle who was younger than he. His grandfather, Isaac Bailey, was a free black man; his grandmother, Betsy Bailey, was owned by Anthony.

On clear blue days, Frederick played in the "bright sunshine, running wild." To Frederick, their windowless cabin with its clay floor and dirt and straw chimney had all the "attractions of a palace." Here, he was loved.

But by the summer of 1824, at age six, Frederick was old enough to work. Betsy had no choice. She took her grandson to the plantation.

If anything, the Wye House, with its long row of white columns in the front, was a palace. It was surrounded by barns, stables, storehouses, tobacco houses, blacksmith shops, kitchens, washhouses, dairies, summerhouses, greenhouses, henhouses, turkey houses, pigeon houses, a huge windmill, and one of the most bountiful gardens in the country. There was a sloop, or sailboat, docked at the river. The poorly built slaves' cabins were set farther back, so as not to disturb the view.

In the 1820s, the Lloyd family owned the Wye House, or Great House. Young Frederick was forced to sleep in a slave cabin.

All of this belonged to Colonel Lloyd. The former governor of Maryland and former U.S. senator owned thirteen farms and hundreds of slaves. Lloyd was assisted by the plantation manager, Aaron Anthony—Frederick's owner.

But no one explained any of this to the young boy. Frederick was left in the kitchen with the slave "Aunt

Katy," who took care of other slave children as well, and was told to sleep in the closet.

In those years, Frederick's chief trouble was "want of food." Aunt Katy used to call the children as if she were calling pigs. Outside, she poured boiled cornmeal in a long trough. The children squatted on the ground and scooped up the mush with oyster shells, pieces of shingle, or their hands. Some days, Aunt Katy didn't feed them anything.

On cold winter nights, Frederick slept in a tow sack as the wind whipped through the boards of the kitchen closet. "My feet have been so cracked with the frost," he wrote later, "that the pen with which I am writing might be laid in the gashes."

Not only did Frederick know hunger and cold; he also knew fear. Once he watched as Master Anthony grabbed Hester, a young slave. Hester was in love with a slave from another farm, and Anthony was angry. He ripped Hester's dress off her back and strung her up from a hook in the kitchen ceiling.

"I'll learn you how to disobey my orders!" he shouted. Over and over, he whipped her.

Frederick was terrified. "I had never seen anything like it before," he wrote. He held his breath, fearing that he would be next.

Because Frederick was too little to do any real work, he did small chores. He drove the cows home in the evening.

A slave is punished by a cold-water treatment while her mistress looks on in approval.

He chased the chickens out of the yard. He ran errands for Master Anthony's daughter, Mrs. Lucretia Auld. She seemed to like the little boy and saved scraps of food for him.

Still, for the most part, Aunt Katy bossed Frederick and made his life miserable. Stay away from the Lloyds' Great House, she warned. Frederick went anyway. He wanted to know how the white people lived.

He played with Daniel, Master Lloyd's young son. Together, they explored the Great House. During Daniel's lessons, Frederick listened and imitated the teacher's cultured, refined voice.

Once Frederick asked, "Why am I a slave?" Because, came the answer, God made black people to be slaves. Frederick did not understand.

In 1826, a turn of events changed Frederick's life. Old and sick, Aaron Anthony retired to one of his own farms. His daughter and her husband moved nearby. Anthony's slaves went with him.

That is, all except Frederick.

2
BALTIMORE SLAVE

On an early Sunday morning in 1826, a sloop docked in the harbor of Baltimore, Maryland. Eight-year-old Frederick stepped off the boat. For the first time in his life, he wore trousers. No doubt, he must have scratched as he stared at the new sights and listened to new sounds.

For whatever reason, Lucretia and Thomas Auld did not want Frederick to become a field slave. Instead, they sent him to Thomas's brother in Baltimore. Here, Frederick lived with Hugh and Sophia Auld and their two-year-old son, Tommy.

Sophia had never been around slaves. She treated

A typical scene of an 1800s harbor, this sailing ship is docked at the wharf while men unload the cargo.

Frederick as she would any child. Frederick was given clean clothes. He slept in a warm straw bed with plenty of covers. He had plenty to eat, much more than the poorer white boys in the neighborhood. When Frederick pointed to words in the Bible, Sophia began to teach him to read.

This, however, was against the law. When Master Hugh found out, he shouted at his wife, "If you teach that nigger [meaning Frederick] how to read, there would be no keeping him. It would forever unfit him to be a slave."

Sophia obeyed her husband. Young Frederick didn't understand, but somehow he sensed that reading was a "pathway" to freedom.

Not too long after Frederick had arrived in Baltimore, his owner, Aaron Anthony, died. Frederick was ordered back to Tuckahoe Creek. Because slaves were property, Frederick and his family stood with the horses, cattle, and pigs as the lawyers decided the worth of each.

Most of Frederick's family became the property of Anthony's son. Frederick, however, remained the property of Lucretia and Thomas Auld. They sent him back to the Aulds, in Baltimore, where he lived for seven years. More than ever, Frederick was determined to learn to read.

Whenever he played with the white boys, he would bring along one of Tommy's old spellers and some bread so that he could trade food for reading lessons.

To learn how to write, Frederick used to tell the boys

that he could write as well as they could. When they said they didn't believe him, Frederick then wrote the letters he knew, and asked them to do better. "In this way I got a good many lessons in writing, which . . . I should never have gotten in any other way."

By shining shoes, he managed to buy his first book, *The Columbian Orator*. One of the speeches in the book was by a slave to his master. Frederick learned those words by heart.

In a way, Master Hugh was right about reading. It did make Frederick unfit to be a slave. The more Frederick learned, the more he was unhappy about his life. He used to tell his white playmates, "You will be free as soon as you are twenty-one, but I am a *slave for life!*"

Frederick wasn't the only person who hated slavery. When he was about thirteen, he began hearing about the work of abolitionists. He didn't know what the word meant, and the dictionary was no help. Finally, after reading a newspaper account of someone praying for the abolition of slavery, Frederick figured out that *abolition* meant "to abolish, or to do away with, slavery." *Abolition* became one of his favorite words.

This New York abolitionist newspaper depicts the horrors of slavery.

EMANCIPATOR—EXTRA.

NEW-YORK, SEPTEMBER 2, 1839.

American Anti-Slavery Almanac for 1840.

The seven cuts following, are selected from thirteen, which may be found in the Anti-Slavery Almanac for 1840. They represent well-authenticated facts, and illustrate in various ways, the cruelties daily inflicted upon three millions of native born Americans, by their fellow-countrymen! A brief explanation follows each cut.

The peculiar "Domestic Institutions of our Southern brethren."

Selling a Mother from her Child.

Mothers with young Children at work in the field.

A Woman chained to a Girl, and a Man in irons at work in the field.

"They can't take care of themselves"; explained in an interesting article.

Hunting Slaves with dogs and guns. A Slave drowned by the dogs.

Servility of the Northern States in arresting and returning fugitive Slaves.

Frederick's teenage years were stormy. He was growing up, becoming more independent, yet angry that he wasn't free. These were powerful emotions, and no doubt, Frederick did not always keep them bottled inside.

Sophia became colder toward Frederick. He was forbidden to read, yet he did it anyway. More than once, in clear view of Sophia, Frederick read at home. Furious, Sophia would grab Frederick's book or newspaper out of his hands.

But this was the least of Frederick's troubles. In 1833, Thomas Auld sent for Frederick. Lucretia had died, and Thomas had married a mean-spirited woman. It was time for Frederick to understand that he was, after all, a *slave for life*.

3
FIELD SLAVE

Thomas Auld was in no mood to be friendly. Slavery was a worrisome business. Auld, just like Frederick, was struggling with complex emotions.

Two years earlier, in 1831, the slave Nat Turner had led a revolt in Virginia, not far from Maryland. Like Frederick, Nat Turner had learned to read and to hate slavery. Turner and a band of slaves killed sixty white people. Turner was hanged.

Thomas Auld was not about to let this happen to Frederick. One way or another, Auld was going to break Frederick's spirit.

Thomas starved Frederick, feeding him nothing but cornmeal mush. He whipped Frederick. Once, when Frederick was teaching slaves to read at Sunday school, Thomas and some men from the church rushed in with sticks and beat them.

Frederick was stubborn. More than once, he deliberately disobeyed Thomas. Some nine months after Frederick arrived, Thomas hired out Frederick as a field hand on Edward Covey's farm. Covey, Frederick wrote, was a "nigger-breaker."

By dawn, the slaves were already at work in the fields. Some nights, they were still working at midnight. "It was never too hot or too cold," wrote Frederick, "or too hard for us to work in the field."

And always, Covey found some reason to beat the slaves. Edward Covey, wrote Frederick, "succeeded in breaking me in body, soul, and spirit."

One Friday in the summer of 1834, Frederick and two other slaves were fanning wheat, separating the kernels of grain. It was Frederick's job to carry the wheat to the fan. In the afternoon heat, Frederick fainted. Work stopped. Covey came running.

Frederick tried to speak. Covey kicked him. Get up, Covey said, kicking Frederick again. Then Covey took a board and hit Frederick in the head. Frederick lay in his own blood.

Most slaves worked long and hard with little food or rest. Here, slaves are unloading rice barges.

That night, Frederick slipped away from Covey's farm. Avoiding roads, Frederick took to the woods and walked five hours to Thomas Auld's store.

Take me home, Frederick pleaded. At first, Thomas seemed concerned. But when he spoke, his voice was cold.

Go back, Thomas told Frederick. If you don't, I'll beat you too.

The next morning, just as Frederick was climbing over Covey's fence to return, Covey raced out with a whip in his hand. Again, Frederick ran.

All day, he hid in the woods. In the evening, Frederick met up with a former slave named Sandy Jenkins. Sandy believed in magic. Keep this root, Sandy said, and no white man will harm you.

On Sunday morning, Frederick arrived at the farm just as Covey headed for church. Surprisingly, Covey waved and went on. Maybe it works, thought Frederick.

Monday morning, Frederick was at work in the barn. He was coming down from the loft when Covey threw a rope around his legs. Frederick fell to the ground. As he struggled to get up, something snapped inside him.

Frederick leaped up at Covey and grabbed him by the throat. The two men struggled. At last, Covey could take no more.

Covey never touched Frederick again. "The battle," Frederick wrote, "was a turning point in my career as a slave."

When the year was up, Thomas hired Frederick to work for William Freeland, in St. Michaels. Freeland was kind for a master, but Frederick had had enough of slavery. He plotted escape.

At a slave auction, men, women, and children stood on the block, while the crowd examined them and placed their bids.

The plan was sketchy, at best. There were five of them: Frederick, Henry Harris, John Harris, Henry Bailey, and Charles Roberts. They planned to head north. Frederick wrote out fake passes that permitted them to travel. On

Good Friday, April 1, 1836, everything was in order. They would leave on Easter.

On Saturday morning, while they were working in the fields, Frederick sensed something was wrong. "We are betrayed," he told Sandy Jenkins. Yes, said Sandy. Frederick always wondered if Sandy had told on them.

The horn called them in for breakfast. Four white men rode up on horseback. Within minutes, the slaves were roped. They were dragged the 15 miles (24 km) to jail.

Frederick was scared. In jail, slave traders looked them over. At the end of the Easter holidays, the other slaves' owners came to get them out of jail. No one came for Frederick.

At home, Thomas paced the floor. He didn't know what to do. Some people in St. Michaels wanted Frederick dead, claiming that he was a troublemaker. Thomas's own wife wanted to sell Frederick and use the money to buy a new house. Frederick wanted his freedom.

One week later, Thomas Auld came for Frederick. I'm sending you back to Baltimore, Thomas told him. Learn a trade. Behave yourself. If you do that, someday I'll give you your freedom.

But Frederick was in no mood to trust a slave owner.

ESCAPE 4

Sounds of shipbuilding filled the Baltimore harbor. There was a rhythm to the clinging, clanging, hammering, and shouting, and Frederick was a part of it. In late spring 1836, right after Frederick arrived in Baltimore, Hugh put Frederick to work at the shipyard.

Frederick learned to caulk ships, filling in the seams of the wooden planks of the boat so that it didn't leak. He enjoyed having a skill and was always proud of his work as a shipbuilder. Frederick earned top wages, yet every penny went straight to Master Hugh.

"Is that all?" Hugh would ask, looking hard as Fred-

An 1830s transatlantic ship is built with heavy oak planks.
At the right, smoking fires are heating tar for caulking.

erick turned over his weekly pay. If Hugh was in a good mood, he would give Frederick a quarter. Frederick felt insulted.

Even in those days, twenty-five cents didn't go very far. Frederick wanted money to buy his freedom and marry. He was in love with Anna Murray, a free black woman who worked as a housekeeper.

30

In August 1838, when Frederick was twenty (but thought he was twenty-one), he went to Hugh. Let me find my own work and my own place to live, he said, and I'll give you part of my wages. Hugh agreed as long as Frederick paid him on Saturday nights. Several weeks later, however, Frederick forgot. By the time Frederick finally showed up on Sunday night, Hugh was furious.

They argued. Hugh demanded that Frederick return home. Frederick obeyed, but the next morning he refused to go to work. By the end of the week, Hugh and Frederick almost came to blows.

With that, Frederick made up his mind. He was going to escape.

For three weeks, Frederick planned. To make sure that Hugh wouldn't suspect anything, Frederick went back to work and turned over his wages to Hugh. This meant that Frederick didn't have enough money for the escape. But Anna Murray did.

Years later, their children claimed that Anna sold her feather bed to pay for Frederick's trip. To travel, Frederick needed an official document. Somehow, he managed to get the papers of a black seaman. Again, Anna helped. She altered Frederick's clothes so that he would look like a sailor.

On Monday morning, September 3, 1838, Frederick was ready. He wore a red shirt and a sailor's hat. At the last minute, Frederick jumped aboard the moving train.

By Jacob Radcliff Mayor, and Richard Riker Recorder, of the City of New-York,

It is hereby Certified, That pursuant to the statute in such case made and provided, we have this day examined *one* certain *male* Negro Slave named *George* the property of *John D_____*

which slave *is* about to be manumitted, and *he* appearing to us to be under forty-five years of age, and of sufficient ability to provide *for himself* we have granted this Certificate, this *twenty fourth* day of *April* in the year of our Lord, one thousand eight hundred and *____*

Jacob Radcliff

R. Riker

Register's Office Lib No 2 of Manumissions page 62
Wm S Slocum Register

Freed slaves carried official documents to show that they were indeed free and were not runaways.

He found a seat in the colored car. (It was the law that blacks had to sit apart from whites.) The conductor came by for tickets and to check the free papers. Frederick's heart beat fast.

The papers in Frederick's pocket described what the seaman looked like, not Frederick. If the conductor read the papers carefully, Frederick would be caught.

"I suppose you have your free papers?" asked the conductor.

Frederick willed himself to stay calm. "No, sir," he replied, "I never carry my free papers to sea with me."

"But you have something to show that you are a free man, have you not?" asked the conductor.

"Yes, sir," Frederick answered. "I have a paper with the American eagle on it, that will carry me round the world."

Frederick pulled out his papers, handing them to the conductor. He held his breath.

The conductor seemed friendly enough. Would he believe that Frederick was really a sailor?

Keeping his eyes on Frederick, the conductor quickly glanced at the papers. The man handed them back, nodded, and went on.

For the moment, Frederick was safe.

Slowly, the steam engine picked up speed. The chugging vibrations did not soothe Frederick's worries. Would a

CAUTION!!

COLORED PEOPLE
OF BOSTON, ONE & ALL,

You are hereby respectfully CAUTIONED and advised, to avoid conversing with the

Watchmen and Police Officers of Boston,

For since the recent ORDER OF THE MAYOR &' ALDERMEN, they are empowered to act as

KIDNAPPERS
AND
Slave Catchers,

And they have already been actually employed in KIDNAPPING, CATCHING, AND KEEPING SLAVES. Therefore, if you value your LIBERTY, and the *Welfare of the Fugitives* among you, *Shun* them in every possible manner, as so many HOUNDS on the track of the most unfortunate of your race.

Keep a Sharp Look Out for KIDNAPPERS, and have TOP EYE open.

APRIL 24, 1851.

Even in the North, blacks were not safe. This Boston advertisement warns colored people to avoid the police.

slave catcher be waiting for him at the end of the line? Sitting in that train, Frederick wrote, "minutes were hours, and hours were days."

Once, after changing trains, Frederick saw a man he knew, a German blacksmith. The man stared at him "intently" before looking away. "I really believe he knew me," Frederick wrote, "but had no heart to betray me."

At Wilmington, Delaware, Frederick took a steamboat to Philadelphia, arriving in midafternoon. With directions from a black porter, Frederick made his way to a ferry, another train, and another ferry. Finally, on Tuesday morning, September 4, 1838, some twenty-four hours after Frederick left Baltimore, he arrived in New York.

"I felt as one might feel upon escape from a den of hungry lions," Frederick wrote home to a friend.

But he wasn't really safe. Watch out, another fugitive (runaway) slave told Frederick. Trust no one. For just a little money, the black people in New York will betray you. "I was without a home," Frederick wrote, "without acquaintances, without money, without credit, without work, and without any definite knowledge as to what course to take. . . . I was indeed free—from slavery, but free from food and shelter as well."

ABOLITIONIST 5

F rederick went into hiding. He sent a message to Anna Murray, telling her how to get to New York. That September, Anna, in a "new plum silk dress," and Frederick, in a suit he had carried in his seaman's bag, were married. Frederick and his bride left for New Bedford, Massachusetts.

For protection, Frederick changed his last name from Bailey to Johnson, but when a friend pointed out there were already many Johnsons, Frederick chose the name Douglas from Walter Scott's poem *Lady of the Lake*, adding an extra "s" on the end. Frederick Augustus Bailey became Frederick Douglass.

This is Anna Murray Douglass, Frederick's first wife.
What emotions do you see in her face?

At first, Frederick worked at any job he could find. Though skilled as a ship caulker, Frederick could not get a job as one because white men refused to work with him. Even in the North there was segregation. Blacks were forbidden to work, live, eat, or sit in certain places.

Still, he and Anna were happy. Their family grew to include five children: Rosetta, Lewis Henry, Frederick, Jr., Charles Redmond, and Annie.

Since Frederick's escape, he had been reading a weekly newspaper called *The Liberator*. Founded in 1831 by two white men who hated slavery—William Lloyd Garrison and Isaac Knapp—this abolitionist paper demanded the emancipation (the freeing) of all slaves. In fact, the closing lines of Garrison's first newspaper article had become famous. "I am in earnest," Garrison wrote, "I will not equivocate—I will not excuse—I will not retreat a single inch—AND I WILL BE HEARD."

Frederick took Garrison's words to heart. On August 16, 1841, he was invited to speak in Nantucket to the Massachusetts Anti-Slavery Society. Frederick was so nervous he stammered. Still, there was something in his words, his face, his entire being, that made everyone in the room sit up and listen. He had spoken the truth.

Frederick had been heard.

Garrison was there, and when Frederick finished he jumped on stage and shouted, "Shall such a man ever be sent back to bondage?" With that, the crowd went wild. They leaped to their feet shouting "No! No! No!"

Never again did Frederick work as a laborer. Eventually, he became one of the greatest American orators, or speakers, of his time. Frederick's voice, deep and expres-

In the 1830s, William Lloyd Garrison called for an immediate end to slavery. Frederick Douglass admired this white man.

Even the masthead of William Lloyd Garrison's famous abolitionist newspaper, *The Liberator*, denounces slavery.

sive, filled the room. Back and forth, Frederick slipped from the sounds of an uneducated slave to the cruel tones of the white master. Tall and handsome, Frederick stood before the crowds and swept them away with his words.

Because of his work with the Anti-Slavery Society, Frederick wasn't home much. Anna, who never learned to read or write, left no record of how she felt about his absence. She didn't join him in the abolitionist movement. Perhaps she felt uncomfortable around his educated friends. Or maybe she was just so busy caring for their children and adding to their income by working at home. No doubt, she missed Frederick.

This daguerreotype catches Frederick's intelligence and intensity. Some whites doubted that he had been a slave.

When Frederick traveled to those meetings, he naturally wanted to sit or eat with the other members of the Anti-Slavery Society. But the laws didn't allow this, because the other members were white. The laws are wrong, said Frederick.

Once, when a train conductor told Frederick to go back to the Negro car, Frederick replied, "If you give me one good reason why I should, I'll go willingly."

"Because you are black!" shouted the conductor.

Frederick did not budge. The conductor and his men pulled; Frederick held on. Ripping the chair from the floor, the men threw it off the train. Frederick went with it, still sitting, still holding onto his seat.

Over the next few years, Frederick gave hundreds of speeches throughout New York, New England, Ohio, and Indiana. When he spoke, Frederick didn't tell where he was from, who owned him, or who had helped him escape.

He didn't want the Aulds to find him, of course, and he wanted to protect the people in the Underground Railroad. (The Underground Railroad was neither underground nor a railroad. It was a group of black and white people who helped runaway slaves, fugitives who traveled at night and hid during the day, escape to the North.)

Crowds found it hard to believe that Frederick had ever been a slave. Stick to your life story, and don't look so smart, the members of the Anti-Slavery Society said. Let the white speakers explain our movement.

Frederick couldn't do it. In June 1845, he wrote and published his first autobiographical book, *Narrative of the Life of Frederick Douglass*. Within three months, it had sold 4,500 copies. Soon it was published in three languages. Within five years, some 30,000 copies had been

Frederick's first autobiography, *Narrative of the Life of Frederick Douglass*, stunned readers and became a best-seller.

sold. Today, the book is considered to be an American classic.

But by telling his story and using real names, Frederick had a problem. Thomas and Hugh Auld could find him. In the fall of 1845, Frederick left the country.

6
CIVIL WAR

Frederick sailed for Great Britain, where slavery had already been abolished. He traveled throughout England, Ireland, Scotland, and Wales, drumming up money for the American cause.

Everywhere it was the same. The crowds loved him. "God bless you, Frederick Douglass!" cried an elderly man. Many people in Britain were already opposed to slavery, but Frederick made many others understand that slavery was wrong.

He stayed almost two years. Perhaps Frederick was afraid of being caught. But it had been years since he had

With dramatic flair, Frederick speaks to an
English audience during his 1846 London visit.

escaped, and not once had Hugh and Thomas Auld tried to capture him, not even after Frederick identified them in his book. Still, as long as Thomas owned Frederick, there was always the possibility that Frederick could be forced back into slavery.

To prevent this from happening, the abolitionist Ellen Richardson purchased Frederick's freedom. Through a lawyer, she offered the Aulds $1,250 for Frederick. They accepted. In the spring of 1847, Frederick came home a free man.

He cherished his independence. On December 3, 1847, in Rochester, New York, the first edition of the newspaper *The North Star* rolled off the press. Frederick was its writer, editor, and publisher.

Over the years, Frederick's life was busy and rewarding. He helped with the Underground Railroad. In 1855, Frederick published his second autobiography, *My Bondage and My Freedom.*

Throughout the country, however, tensions were mounting. There was talk of war.

On October 16, 1859, John Brown and twenty-two men seized the U.S. Arsenal in Harpers Ferry (now in West Virginia). Brown planned to steal weapons, arm slaves, and then invade the South. On October 18, General Robert E. Lee captured Brown and his men.

With Brown in jail waiting for a trial, the governor of

Describe what is happening in this undated painting, *The Underground Railroad*.

Before his hanging, the radical abolitionist kisses a black child in the *Last Moments of John Brown* by Thomas Hovendon.

Virginia, Henry Wise, went looking for Brown's allies. I'm not only going to hang Brown, said the governor (which he did); I want the arrest of Frederick Douglass.

In less than a month, Frederick was on a ship sailing for England. But that spring, when his daughter Annie died, Frederick came home, in spite of the danger.

Frederick plunged into his work. He supported the newly formed Republican party, hoping that Abraham Lincoln would become president and free the slaves.

The country moved closer to war. Some southern plantation owners claimed that the issue was not slavery, but states' rights. States, they said, should have more power than the federal government.

In December 1860, soon after Lincoln's election, South Carolina seceded (withdrew) from the Union. In January, six more states seceded. On April 12, 1861, southern troops fired on Fort Sumter. The Civil War had begun.

Many claimed that it was a war to free the slaves. But it was more complicated than that. Privately Lincoln believed that slavery was wrong, but publicly he said little. Lincoln knew that many white people wouldn't fight to free blacks. This war, declared Lincoln, was to preserve the Union.

On January 1, 1863, however, Lincoln announced the Emancipation Proclamation. "I never saw such joy before," Frederick wrote. Still, not a single slave was actually freed.

A. A. Lamb includes patriotic emblems in his painting of the Emancipation Proclamation. President Lincoln is at the right.

When the North was losing, blacks were allowed to enlist in the Army. Black soldiers were paid less than whites. They were given the toughest positions to defend. In spite of this unfairness, Frederick's sons, Charles and Lewis, were the first to join the Army in New York.

It seemed that the killing and destruction would never stop. But finally, on April 9, 1865, the southern forces surrendered. The war was over, with more Americans killed than in any war before or since. Even today, there remains a trace of bitterness and grief.

With their goal accomplished, the Anti-Slavery Society disbanded. Frederick didn't know what to do with himself. "I felt I had reached the end of the noblest and best part of my life," he wrote. "Where shall I go?"

FINAL 7 YEARS

Frederick Douglass was the most famous black man in the world. He served as the first black U.S. marshall and the first black ambassador to Haiti, and he was appointed to the position of recorder of deeds. These were great honors, but they were ceremonial at best; Frederick had little power.

He seemed to realize that his greatness was in large part based on his own life story. For the third and last time, Frederick rewrote and published his autobiography, *Life and Times of Frederick Douglass.*

In the years that followed the Civil War, everyone

Frederick serves as a U.S. Marshall at
President Garfield's inauguration.

seemed to have a solution to the "Negro problem," and Frederick was no different. Sometimes his decisions were good, and sometimes they weren't. When hundreds of former slaves headed for Kansas, Frederick claimed that they should stay put in the South and confront their problems.

Yet Frederick had not done that; he had escaped. Black audiences booed him.

In 1874, he became the president of the first bank for blacks, the Freedman's Savings and Trust in Washington, D.C. Unfortunately, as a result of bad loans, thousands of the bank's depositors lost their entire savings. Frederick had neglected to check the bank's records.

In June 1877, sixty-year-old Frederick returned home to Talbot County, Maryland, for a visit. Thomas Auld, his former owner, was dying.

They had not seen or spoken to one another for nearly forty years. They greeted each other stiffly, and then Thomas started to cry. Silently, the two old men sat together, hand in hand. At last Frederick spoke. What do you think about my running away, he asked.

"Frederick," Thomas answered softly, "I always knew

Frederick was the president of the first bank for blacks, the Freedman's Saving and Trust Company.

you were too smart to be a slave, and had I been in your place, I should have done the same as you did."

Time marched on. On August 4, 1882, Anna died. Whatever differences they might have had, Frederick was heartbroken. Still, two years later, he quietly married forty-five-year-old Miss Helen Pitts. Helen was white.

Few people approved of Frederick's marriage. Even his children were rude to him. For Frederick, however, it was never the person's color that was important; it was the person.

In the summer of 1893, Frederick gave a speech at the World's Fair in Chicago. When the old man stood, he fumbled with his glasses and with his papers. He mumbled. White men in the back jeered at him.

For a moment, Frederick looked confused. Then, throwing his speech and his glasses aside, he ran his hands through his thick white hair. The old Frederick came roaring back.

"Men talk of the race problem," he thundered. "There is no Negro problem. The problem is whether the American people have loyalty enough, honor enough, patriotism enough, to live up to their own Constitution."

On February 20, 1895, at a meeting in Washington, D.C., Frederick spoke in favor of women's rights. (Until 1920, women were not allowed to vote.) Susan B. Anthony presided. Afterward, one British delegate described

Frederick and Helen Pitts Douglass pose for a picture on their honeymoon to Niagara Falls.

Americans honor Frederick Douglass,
a famous patriot.

Frederick "as a commanding figure six feet [183 cm] high, a splendid head with large and well-formed features, soft, pathetic eyes, complexion of olive-brown, flowing white hair."

That evening, Frederick entertained Helen by imitating the voices of the delegates who had been at the meeting. Since those early days on Tuckahoe Creek, Frederick had always mimicked the sounds of animals and people. With a grand flourish, Frederick rose from his chair, collapsed, and died.

He was buried in Rochester, in the family plot, next to Anna.

Frederick Augustus Bailey Douglass never planned to be the most famous black man in the world. He just wanted to be free. "Once you learn to read," Frederick wrote, "you will be forever free." For untold numbers of Americans, his story had made all the difference.

FOR FURTHER READING

Archer, Jules. *They Had a Dream: The Civil Rights Struggle, from Frederick Douglass to Marcus Garvey to Martin Luther King, Jr. and Malcolm X.* New York: Viking, 1993.

Banta, Melissa. *Frederick Douglass.* New York: Chelsea Juniors, 1993.

Bennett, Evelyn. *Frederick Douglass and the War Against Slavery.* Brookfield, Conn.: Millbrook Press, 1993.

Douglass, Frederick, and Michael McCurdy. *Escape from Slavery: The Boyhood of Frederick Douglass in His Own Words*. New York: Knopf, 1994.

McFeely, William S. *Frederick Douglass*. New York: Simon and Schuster, 1992.

McKissack, Patricia and Fredrick. *Frederick Douglass: Leader Against Slavery*. Hillside, N.J.: Enslow Publishers, 1991.

Miller, Douglas T. *Frederick Douglass and the Fight for Freedom*. New York: Facts on File, 1993.

Patterson, Lillie, and Gary Morrow. *Frederick Douglass, Freedom Fighter*. New York: Chelsea Junior, 1991

Weiner, Eric. *The Story of Frederick Douglass, Voice of Freedom*. New York: Dell, 1992.

INDEX

Abolition, 20
Abolitionists, 20, 38, 40, 46
Anthony, Aaron, 10, 11, 14, 16, 19
Anthony, Susan B., 55
Anti-Slavery Society, 38, 40, 41, 42, 51
Auld, Hugh, 17, 19, 20, 29, 31, 42, 43, 46
Auld, Lucretia, 16, 17, 19, 22
Auld, Sophia, 17, 19, 22

Auld, Thomas, 17, 19, 22, 23–24, 25, 26, 28, 42, 43, 46, 54

Bailey, Betsy (grandmother), 7, 9, 12
Bailey, Harriet (mother), 11
Bailey, Henry, 27
Bailey, Isaac (grandfather), 12
Baltimore (Maryland), 17, 28, 29, 35

Brown, John, 46

Chicago World's Fair, 55
Civil War, 49, 51, 52
Covey, Edward, 24, 26

Douglass, Anna Murray (first wife), 30, 31, 36, 40, 55, 58
Douglass, Annie, 38, 49
Douglass, Charles Redmond, 38, 51
Douglass, Frederick
  ambassador to Haiti, 52
  and Anti-Slavery Society, 38, 40, 41, 42, 51
  appearance, 57
  autobiographies, 42–43, 46, 52
  in Baltimore, 17–22, 29–33
  birth, 11
  "broken" by Edward Covey, 24
  childhood, 7–20
  condemns slavery, 9
  death, 58
  in England, 44, 49
  flees slavery, 26–28, 31–35
  heads Freedman's Savings and Trust, 54
  learns to read, 19–20, 22, 58
  marriages, 36, 55
  as public speaker, 38–40, 42, 54, 55
  publishes *The North Star*, 46
  purchases freedom, 46
  as shipbuilder, 29, 37
  as U.S. Marshall, 52
Douglass, Frederick, Jr. (son), 38
Douglass, Helen Pitts (second wife), 55
Douglass, Lewis (son), 38, 51
Douglass, Rosetta (daughter), 38

Emancipation Proclamation, 49

Freedman's Savings and Trust, 54
Freeland, William, 26

Garrison, William Lloyd, 38

Harris, Henry, 27
Harris, John, 27

Jenkins, Sandy, 26, 28

Katy, Aunt, 13, 14, 16
Knapp, Isaac, 38

Lee, Robert E., 46
Liberator, The, 38
Life and Times of Frederick Douglass, 52
Lincoln, Abraham, 49
Lloyd, Colonel Edward, 10, 13, 16

Maryland, 23
My Bondage and My Freedom, 46

Narrative of the Life of Frederick Douglass, 42–43
New Bedford (Massachusetts), 36
New York, New York, 35, 36
North Star, The, 46

Republican Party, 49
Richardson, Ellen, 46
Roberts, Charles, 27
Rochester (New York), 46, 58
Runaway slaves, 42

Segregation, 37
Slavery, 9, 20, 23, 46, 49

Talbot County (Maryland), 11, 54
Turner, Nat, 23

Underground Railroad, 42

Women's rights, 55

ABOUT THE AUTHOR

Mona Kerby, a Texan, now lives in Maryland, the state where Frederick Douglass lived as a boy. Kerby teaches at Western Maryland College in Westminster. She, her husband, Steve, and their dog named Sam currently live in an eighteenth century farmhouse, previously owned by the famous Dante scholar Charles Singleton.